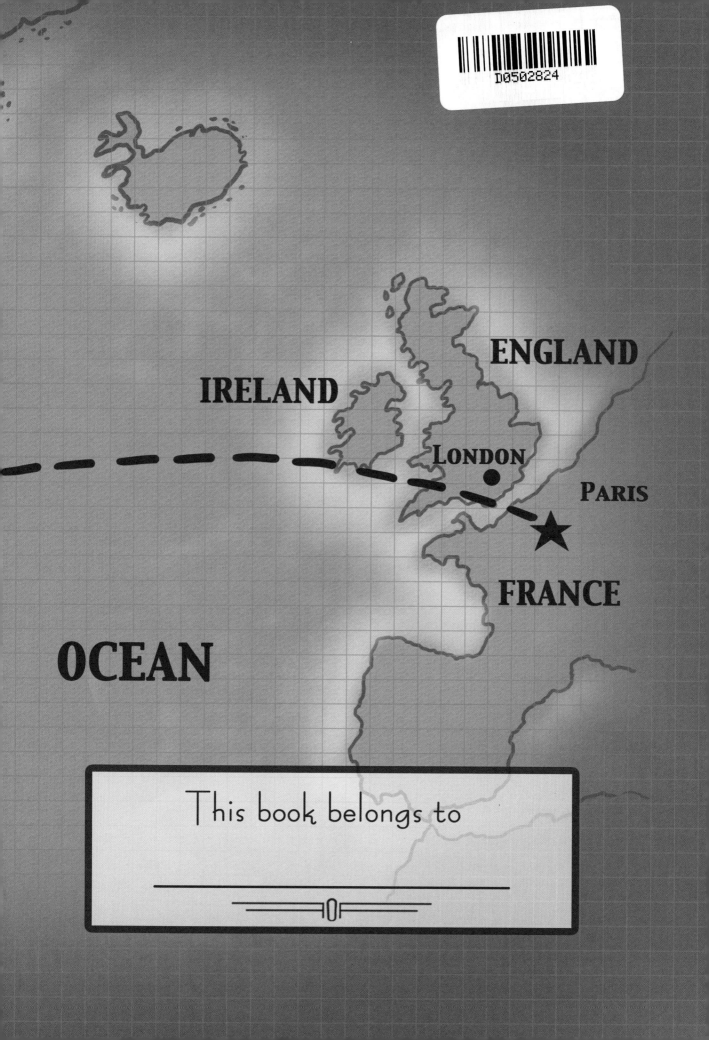

ENGLAND

IRELAND

LONDON

PARIS

FRANCE

OCEAN

The Spirit of Lindy

Story, Concept & Characters by
Kermit Weeks

Premise Entertainment Artists

Pencils
Dominic Carola
Paint
Ryan Feltman

To
Oscar + Boris,
To KNOW what's
beyond the horizon...
You must GO
beyond the horizon!

To all those
standing before a vast ocean
with their sights set on a distant shore.

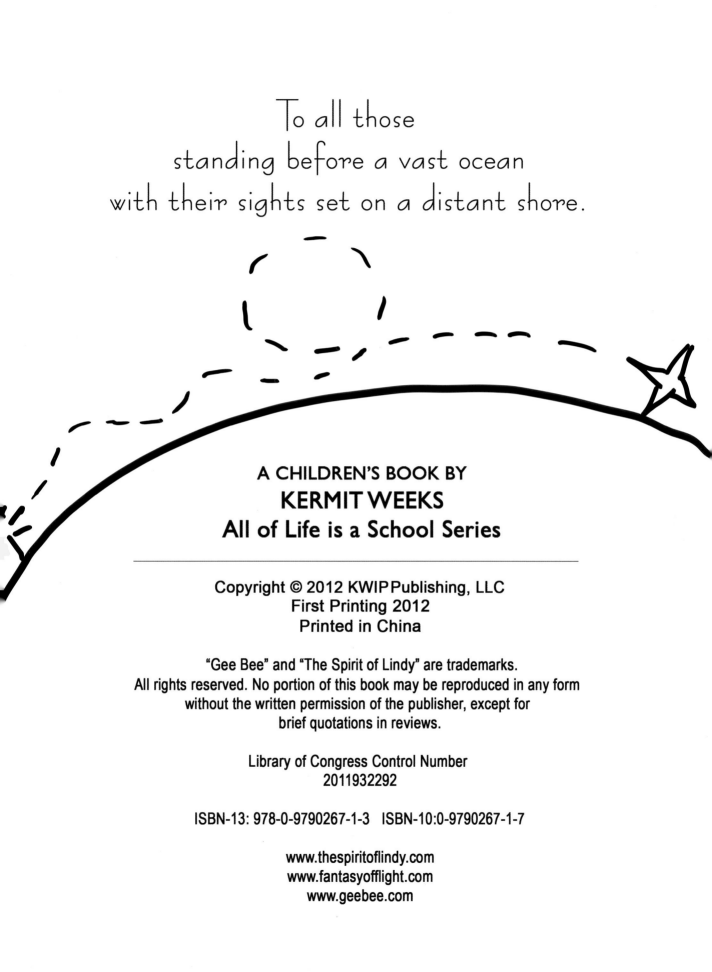

A CHILDREN'S BOOK BY
KERMIT WEEKS
All of Life is a School Series

Library of Congress Control Number
2011932292

ISBN-13: 978-0-9790267-1-3   ISBN-10:0-9790267-1-7

www.thespiritoflindy.com
www.fantasyofflight.com
www.geebee.com

It's a beautiful morning over a seemingly never-ending countryside, as a lone mail plane named Geoffrey D. H. flies along in the sunlit skies.

Such is the life of the planes that carry the mail . . . day, after day, after day. But this day is different . . . Geoffrey is excited . . . for he has a grand idea!

As the Fantasy of Flight airfield begins to awaken to its daily activities, Geoffrey arrives in the morning light. Bursting with excitement, he can hardly wait to share his enthusiasm.

Zee chimes in, "Maybe we could build one . . . a special one . . . that *could* make it?"
Puff adds, "I'll bet the shop tools could do it!"

Puff gets excited, "OK, Zee and I will go talk to the owner while the rest of you go see what the shop tools think."

Everyone looks on in anticipation as Curtiss asks,
"Do you think it can be done?"

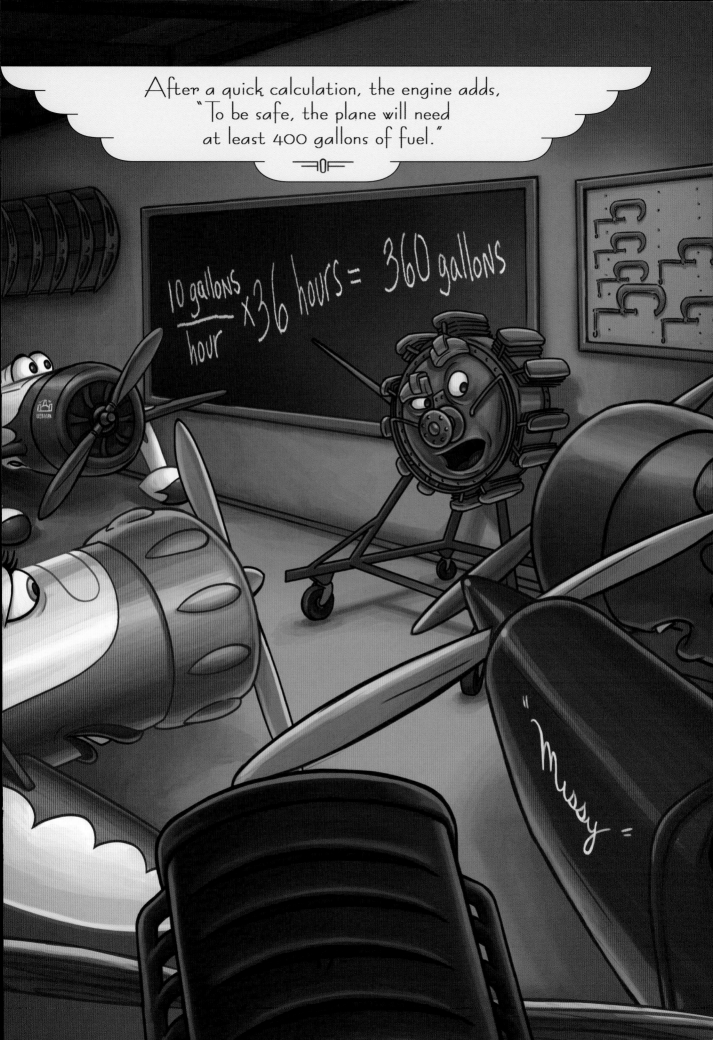

while Buzz, Planer, Jointer, and Sander make the wing.

-22-

Puff announces, "Let's call *him* Lindy!"
Everyone agrees, and his new name is painted on the cowling.

Geoffrey arrives with the latest newspaper showing that others have attempted to claim the prize but have failed. Missy comments quietly, "Maybe we should have called him *Lucky Lindy!*"

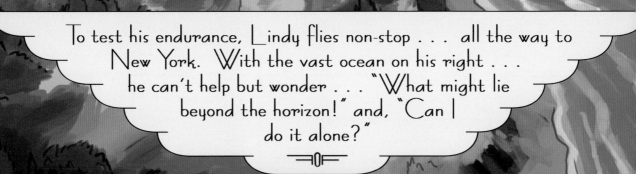

To test his endurance, Lindy flies non-stop . . . all the way to New York. With the vast ocean on his right . . . he can't help but wonder . . . "What might lie beyond the horizon!" and, "Can I do it alone?"

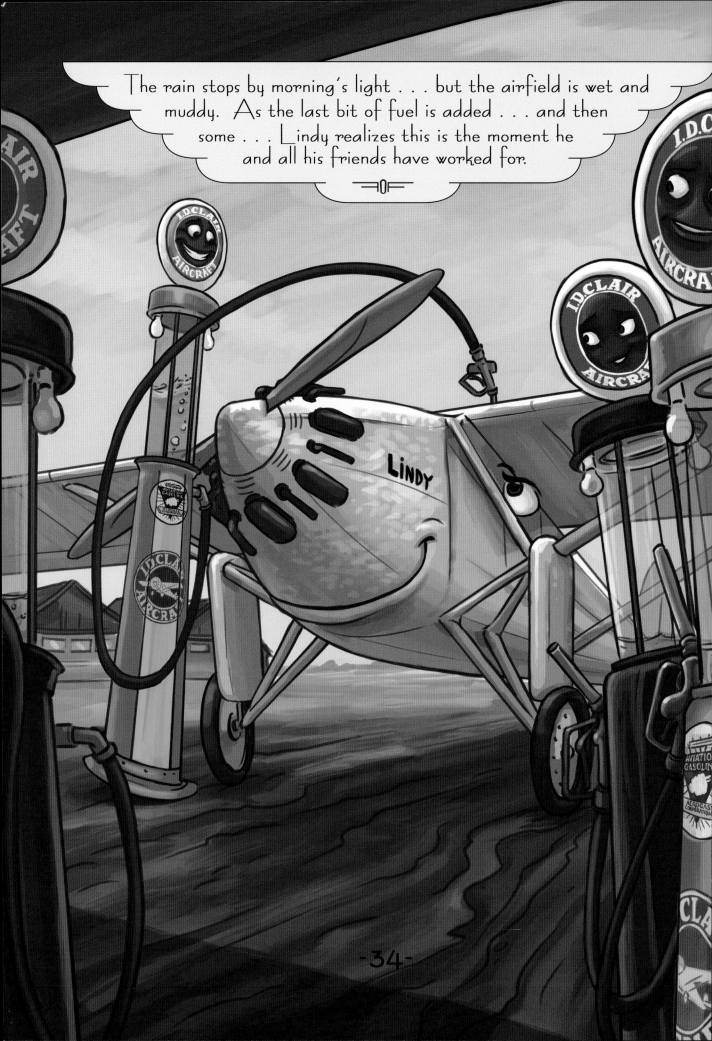

Sluggish at first . . . he slowly picks up speed. Struggling to get airborne . . . he bounces several times. Full of fuel . . . and knowing the end of the runway is fast approaching . . . he shudders to think what might happen if he fails!

-38-

The first part of the journey has Lindy flying over land and water.
Leaving land, he quickly loses sight of the shoreline.
"I'd better get used to this!"
Looking down, he suddenly realizes . . .
"I don't know how to swim!"

Flying over water, Lindy holds his heading . . . making slight adjustments after checking his drift by watching the wind blow spray off the tops of waves. Over the land, he dodges mountains and rain showers, checking his course with the landmarks below.

As the sun begins to set, Lindy buzzes low over the last town he will see for a very long time. A sense of loneliness overcomes him as he heads out over the vast ocean before him. Darkness will be upon him soon.

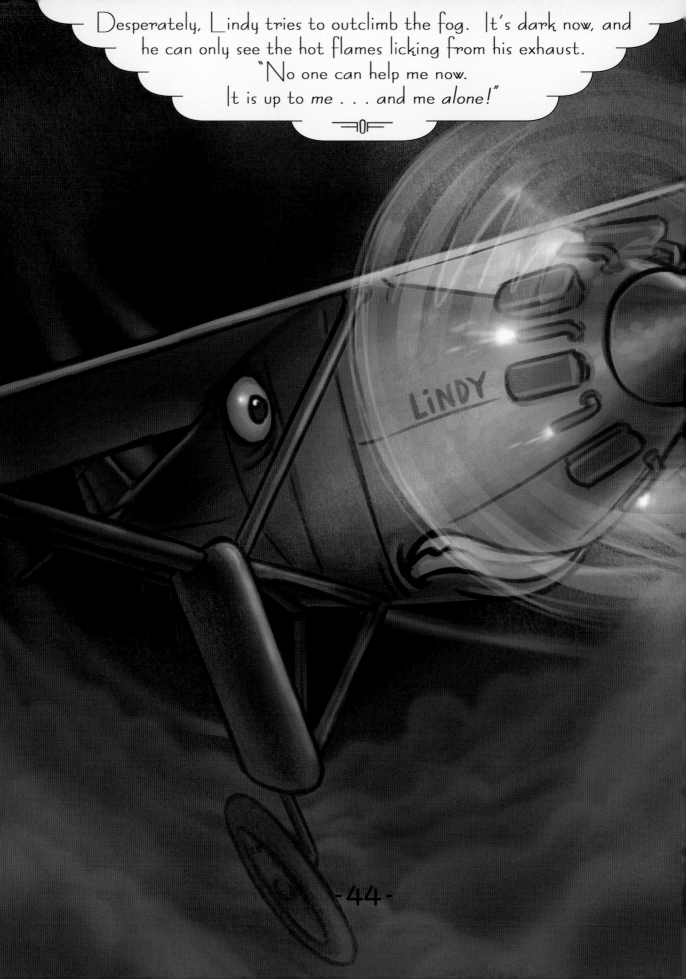

Finally, Lindy is able to get above the fog and sighs with relief as stars appear above him. He can use them for navigation. Looking down, he thinks, "If I went down now . . . into the icy waters below . . . *no one would ever find me!*"

Hours and hours pass . . . as Lindy struggles to stay awake. His heading wanders . . . and it becomes increasingly difficult to hold his altitude. Now flying at 10,000 feet, it is much harder to breathe . . . only adding to his drowsiness.

Thinking it's his imagination, Lindy begins to sense, huge, dark, shapes. Squinting to make them out, a flash of lightning reveals they're GIANT STORMS! With resolve he decides, "I must hold my heading. I must stay on course!"

While fighting off the cold . . . and trying to stay awake . . .
he notices a brightening horizon. It's the moon rising . . .
and it becomes easier to see the storms!
Now, at the halfway point, Lindy knows
he can no longer turn back . . .
He *must* continue on!

But Lindy is sooooo tired. With the drone of his engine . . .
and the monotony of flying on and on and on . . .
it's all he can do to keep his eyes open.
He knows . . . it will only get worse!

The voice within reassures him . . . encourages him . . .
advises him . . . and guides him. "Stay awake! . . .
Don't give up! . . . Stay on course! . . .
You can do it! . . . You have a Destiny!"

Lost in an inner world, Lindy suddenly bursts from a cloud to see white caps below and a bright sun on the horizon! With new energy he realizes . . . he has made it through the darkness!

Flying low, Lindy circles and yells, "Which way is Ireland?"
They happily point the way!

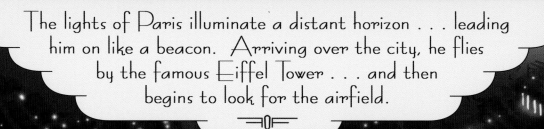

The lights of Paris illuminate a distant horizon . . . leading
him on like a beacon. Arriving over the city, he flies
by the famous Eiffel Tower . . . and then
begins to look for the airfield.

Back at Fantasy of Flight . . . everyone crowds around a radio to hear the announcement: "Lucky Lindy, as they call him, landed at the Paris Airfield this evening . . . arriving from New York!" Everyone is ecstatic!

Lindy returns by ship and is everyone's hero. Many of his airplane friends and fans greet him at the harbor for a spectacular "Welcome Home!"

All the planes nod in agreement . . . and decide there is just one last touch that now seems appropriate. Paintbrush goes to work on Lindy's cowl . . . and from this day forward . . . he is forever known as the *SPIRIT OF LINDY!*

The
Journey
Continues . . .

An Attraction on a Higher Plane

Polk County (Orlampa), Florida

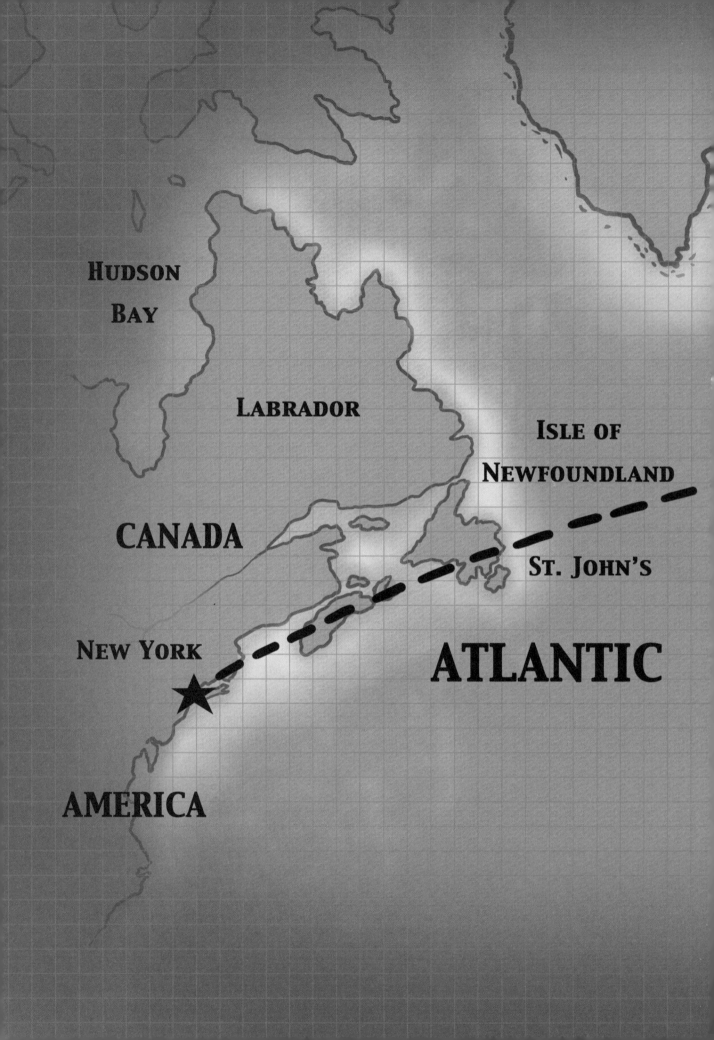